Dear Parent:

Congratulations! Your child is taking the first steps on an exciting journey. The destination? Independent reading!

STEP INTO READING® will help your child get there. The program offers five steps to reading success. Each step includes fun stories and colorful art. There are also Step into Reading Sticker Books, Step into Reading Math Readers, Step into Reading Write-In Readers, Step into Reading Phonics Readers, and Step into Reading Phonics First Steps! Boxed Sets—a complete literacy program with something for every child.

Learning to Read, Step by Step!

Ready to Read Preschool–Kindergarten
• big type and easy words • rhyme and rhythm • picture clues
For children who know the alphabet and are eager to begin reading.

Reading with Help Preschool–Grade 1
• basic vocabulary • short sentences • simple stories
For children who recognize familiar words and sound out new words with help.

Reading on Your Own Grades 1–3
• engaging characters • easy-to-follow plots • popular topics
For children who are ready to read on their own.

Reading Paragraphs Grades 2–3
• challenging vocabulary • short paragraphs • exciting stories
For newly independent readers who read simple sentences with confidence.

Ready for Chapters Grades 2–4
• chapters • longer paragraphs • full-color art
For children who want to take the plunge into chapter books but still like colorful pictures.

STEP INTO READING® is designed to give every child a successful reading experience. The grade levels are only guides. Children can progress through the steps at their own speed, developing confidence in their reading, no matter what their grade.

Remember, a lifetime love of reading starts with a single step!

Visit us on the Web!
www.stepintoreading.com
www.barbie.com

Educators and librarians, for a variety of teaching tools, visit us at
www.randomhouse.com/teachers

Library of Congress Cataloging-in-Publication Data
Parker, Jessie.
Horse show champ / by Jessie Parker ; illustrated by Karen Wolcott. — 1st ed.
  p. cm. — (Step into reading. Step 1 book)
At head of title: Barbie
ISBN: 978-0-375-84701-1 (trade)—ISBN: 978-0-375-94701-8 (lib. bdg.)
I. Wolcott, Karen. II. Title. III. Title: Barbie.   PZ7.K5553Hor 2009   2006036319

Printed in the United States of America
30 29 28 27 26 25 24 23 22 21 20
First Edition

Barbie™

Horse Show Champ

By Jessie Parker

Illustrated by Karen Wolcott

Random House 🏠 New York

Barbie pops out of bed.

The horse show is today!

Barbie eats

a big breakfast.

She grabs an apple.

It is for her horse.

Tawny loves apples!

Barbie brushes Tawny.
What a shiny mane!

Barbie braids her tail.
She ties a red bow.

"I hope we win

a blue ribbon today!"

Barbie puts
on her
horse show
outfit.

Her boots are shiny.

Her hair is braided.

"We match!" she says.

Barbie and Tawny
are led into the ring.

They walk.

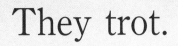

They trot.

They gallop.

Now they must jump.

Tawny is scared.

She goes

around the fence.

"Jump for me, Tawny," says Barbie.

"I have an apple
for you."

Tawny tries again.

She jumps over the bar.

They did it!

Hooray!

A white ribbon
for Barbie.

A red apple for Tawny!